Library of Congress Cataloging-in-Publication Data
Martin, Bill, 1916–
Chicken Chuck / by Bill Martin Jr and Bernard Martin; illustrated by Steven Salerno.—1st ed.
p.   cm.
Summary: Chicken Chuck the rooster, who has set himself up as boss of the barnyard by virtue of the special blue feather
in the middle of his forehead, finds his authority undermined by a circus horse with two blue feathers.
ISBN: 1-890817-31-7
[1. Individuality—Fiction. 2. Roosters—Fiction. 3. Domestic animals—Fiction. 4. Circus—Fiction.]
I. Martin, Bernard, 1912–1998. II. Salerno, Steven, ill. III. Title.
zPZ7.M3643 Ch 2000
[E]—dc21
99-37956   CIP

Creative Director: Bretton Clark
Designer: Rose Walsh
Editor: Margery Cuyler

The illustrations in this book were prepared using mixed media.
Printed in Belgium
First hardcover edition, 04/00
First paperback edition, 09/01

2 4 6 8 10 9 7 5 3 1

WINSLOW PRESS

Home Office: All inquiries:
770 East Atlantic Ave.   115 East 23rd Street
Suite 201   10th Floor
Delray Beach, FL 33483   New York, NY 10010

Discover *Chicken Chuck*'s interactive Web site with worldwide links, games, activities, and more at:
winslowpress.com

Chicken Chuck

To Maxine Martin with fond remembrances of
her husband and my brother, Bernard
—*BM Jr*

For Patricia Ann
—*Steve*

WINSLOW PRESS

Delray Beach, Florida • New York

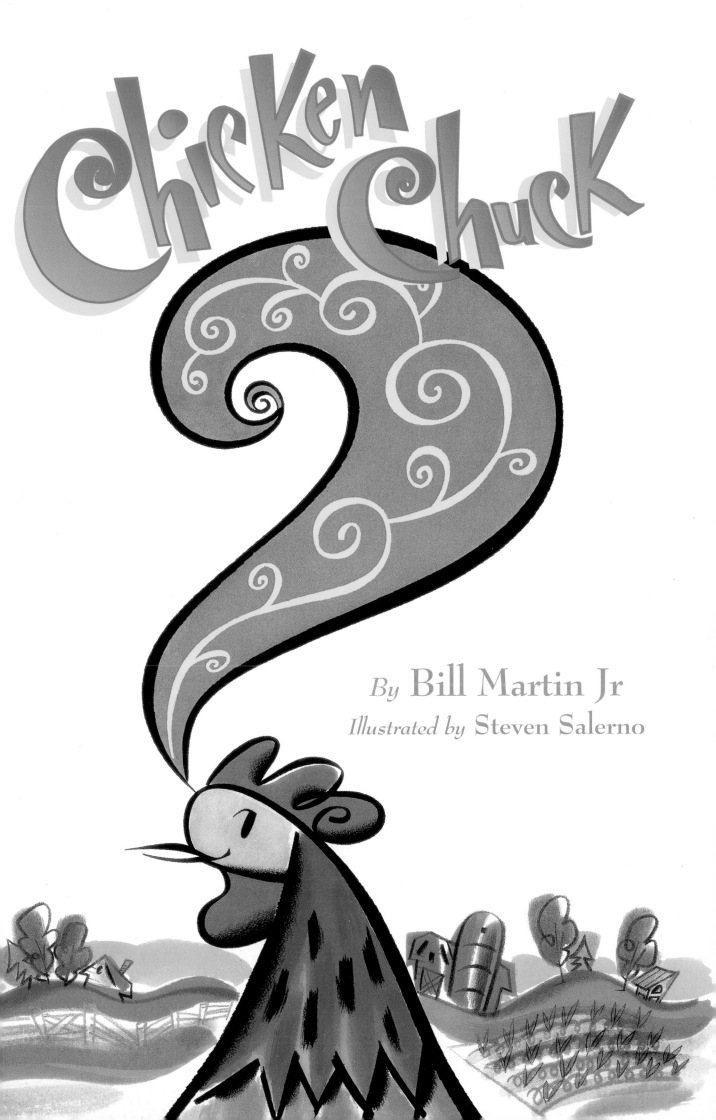

Chicken Chuck

By Bill Martin Jr

Illustrated by Steven Salerno

A rooster named Chicken Chuck lived
in a model barnyard.
    More than anything, he liked to eat.
He had three meals a day and snacks in between.

One day, Chicken Chuck found a big **blue seed** in the farmyard. When he ate it, a strange thing happened.

A bright blue feather sprouted right in the middle of his forehead.

It grew, and grew, and grew!

"Where did you get that feather?"
cackled Henna the Hen. "I want one, too."
"I ate a seed," crowed Chicken Chuck,
"and this bright blue feather sprouted."

"I like that feather," hissed Necky the Goose.

"Me, too!" grunted Blimpy the Pig.

"I want one like that," brayed Donnie the Donkey.

"I eat seeds," said the Butterfat Cow, "but I don't have a feather on my head."

"This was a special seed," Chicken Chuck said proudly. "Perhaps you will find one, too."

So everyone gobbled seeds and waited for
blue feathers to sprout. Nothing happened.
Chicken Chuck chuckled, "I'm the boss of the
barnyard, for only *I* have a bright blue feather."
And he became very bossy indeed.

He made Necky the Goose wash her neck.

He made Blimpy the Pig curl the little pigs' tails.

He made Donnie the Donkey wash his ears.

He made Pluck the Duck give the ducklings a bath every morning.

And he made the little chicks hold in their fat little gizzards.

One morning, a man came to the farmyard and pasted a poster on the barn. It was a picture of circus animals and circus clowns. "See here! See here!" hissed Necky the Goose. "The white horse in the picture has TWO blue feathers on his head. He's even more handsome than Chicken Chuck!"

"Even more handsome than Chicken Chuck!" echoed Pluck the Duck and Blimpy the Pig. Everyone in the barnyard admired the circus horse. He had TWO blue feathers. Chicken Chuck had only one.

"Oh, drumsticks!" screamed Chicken Chuck.
"That can't be true. Feathers don't grow on horses."
"Perhaps they do," said the Butterfat Cow. "That
horse may have eaten a blue seed like the one you ate."

Chicken Chuck slunk into the henhouse. His bright blue feather drooped. For days he gulped seeds hoping to sprout a second blue feather . . . but that feather didn't sprout.

One morning at half-past daybreak, Chicken Chuck stormed out of the henhouse. "I'm going to the circus," he squawked. "We shall see if that horse *really* has feathers on his head."

Everyone followed Chicken Chuck as he strutted to the circus. There he saw the tigers and the lions and the bears. He saw a giraffe and an elephant, but he didn't see a white horse with blue feathers on his head.

"Well, clabber milk," said the Butterfat Cow. "Look here!"
Everyone crowded around to see a little monkey fast asleep.
"Wake up, you!" screamed Chicken Chuck. "Where can I
find the white horse with blue feathers on his head?"

Achoo! Achoo!

The monkey blinked and
began to sneeze. "Achoo! Achoo! Achoo!
Blue feathers make me sneeze," he said. "*Achoo!*"

He grabbed Chicken Chuck's bright blue feather.

Chicken Chuck squawked. He hopped. He bucked.

He flapped his wings and screeched. The monkey held on. Quick as a flash, he pulled

out Chicken Chuck's bright blue feather. He threw it as far as he could.

"My feather! My bright
blue feather!" squawked Chicken
Chuck. "You pulled out my bright
blue feather!"
"I'm sorry," sneezed the monkey as tears rolled down
his cheeks. "I don't . . . Achoo! . . . don't . . . Achoo! . . .
I don't like blue feathers. They make me cough!
They make me sneeze!"
Chicken Chuck began to cry.

"Don't be sad," said the monkey. "I can give you lots of blue feathers."

"You can?" shouted Donnie the Donkey and Blimpy the Pig and Pluck the Duck. "Can you give each of us a blue feather?"

"Yes. Come with me," wheezed the monkey. "But I warn you, I may sneeze some more."

Everyone followed the monkey to the white horse's stall.

"Look!" screamed Chicken Chuck. "There is the white horse. He does have TWO blue feathers . . . but they are tied on his head!"

"Of course," sneezed the monkey. "Here is a box of blue feathers like those the white horse wears. Please take all these blue feathers back to your barnyard. Achoo!"

Now the model barnyard is a mass of bobbing feathers. Pluck the Duck, Henna the Hen, Necky the Goose, Blimpy the Pig— even Donnie the Donkey and the Butterfat Cow—wear bright blue feathers . . . right in the middle of their foreheads!

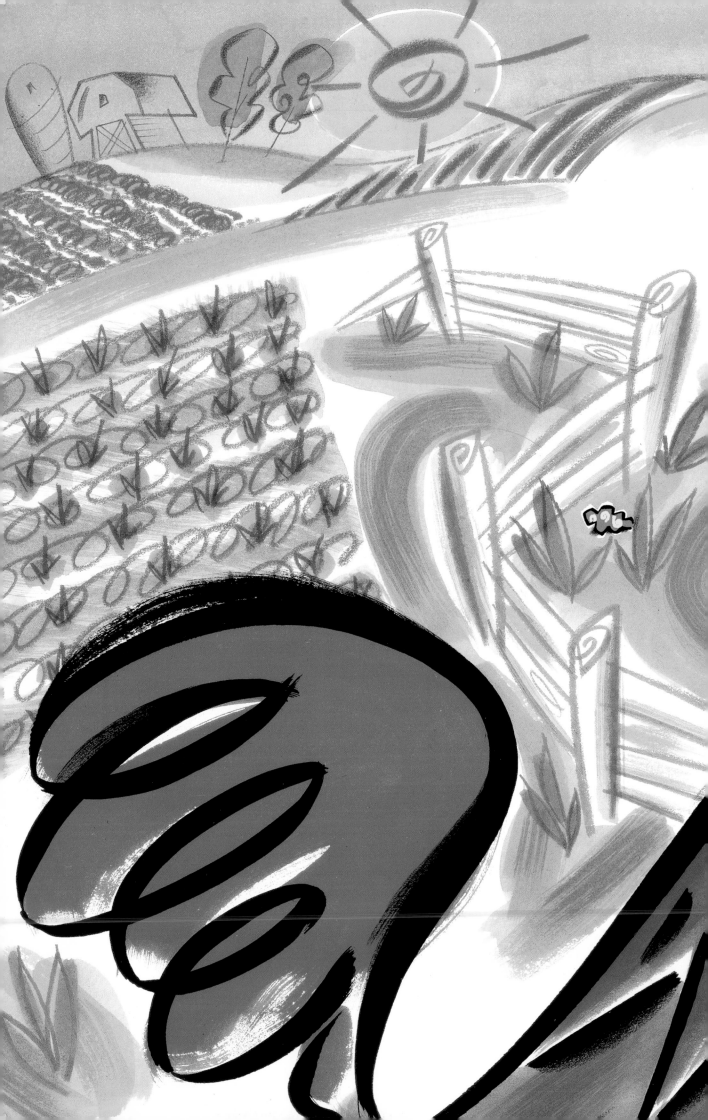

Chicken Chuck wears two blue feathers, but he isn't satisfied. He hopes someday he'll find another blue seed that will make a blue feather sprout . . . right in the middle of his forehead!